The Wishing-Well Spell

To my auntie Wawie,
the most adventurous spirit
and traveler
—G. S.

#6

Daisy Dreamer

The Wishing-Well Spell

By Holly Anna • Illustrated by Genevieve Santos

LITTLE SIMON

New York London Toronto Sydney New Delhi

LITTLE SIMON

An imprint of Simon & Schuster Children's Publishing Division
1230 Avenue of the Americas, New York, New York 10020
First Little Simon paperback edition April 2018
Copyright © 2018 by Simon & Schuster, Inc.
Also available in a Little Simon hardcover edition.
All rights reserved, including the right of reproduction in whole or in part in any form.
LITTLE SIMON is a registered trademark of Simon & Schuster, Inc., and associated colophon is a trademark of Simon & Schuster, Inc. For information about special discounts for bulk purchases, please contact Simon & Schuster Special Sales at 1-866-506-1949 or business@simonandschuster.com. The Simon & Schuster Speakers Bureau can bring authors to your live event. For more information or to book an event contact the Simon & Schuster Speakers Bureau at 1-866-248-3049 or visit our website at www.simonspeakers.com.
Designed by Laura Roode
Manufactured in the United States of America 1021 MTN
4 6 8 10 9 7 5
Library of Congress Cataloging-in-Publication Data
Names: Anna, Holly, author. | Santos, Genevieve, illustrator.
Title: The wishing-well spell / by Holly Anna ; illustrated by Genevieve Santos.
Description: First Little Simon paperback edition. | New York : Little Simon, 2018. | Series: Daisy Dreamer ; 6 | Summary: When Daisy Dreamer's imaginary friend, Posey, repairs a wishing well, suddenly every wish made since it was broken comes true.
Identifiers: LCCN 2017023263 | ISBN 9781534412651 (pbk) | ISBN 9781534412668 (hc) | ISBN 9781534412675 (eBook)
Subjects: | CYAC: Wishes—Fiction. | Imagination—Fiction. | Imaginary playmates—Fiction. | Friendship—Fiction. | BISAC: JUVENILE FICTION / Imagination & Play. | JUVENILE FICTION / Humorous Stories. | JUVENILE FICTION / Readers / Chapter Books.
Classification: LCC PZ7.1.A568 Wis 2018 | DDC [Fic]—dc23
LC record available at https://lccn.loc.gov/2017023263

CONTENTS

CHAPTER ONE

Park Day!

Today is Friday, and that means it's park day!

My best friends and I go to the park every Friday after school. Today we head straight to the basketball court.

I love the court because it's the best place to *ro-o-oll* on my skateboard. Lily loves it because it's the best place

to play basketball. And Jasmine loves it because it's the best place to draw on the smooth surface with sidewalk chalk. It's the perfect place for us. *Obviously.*

I slalom around Lily. *ZOOMIE! ZOOM! ZOOM!* She dunks a three-pointer or whatever.

I whiz past Jasmine. *ZOOMIE! ZOOM! ZOOM!* She's drawing a picture of Posey.

"Hi, Posey!" I shout as I fly by.

The picture of Posey pops to life—as in, *real* life.

"Hi, guys!" he shouts back.

I'm so distracted that I skate right into Lily.

WIPEOUT!

Lily and I bumble-tumble to the ground.

"Oopsy-daisy!" I cry. Lily and I untangle ourselves and check for scrapes.

"Are you okay?" everyone asks at the *exact same time*!

"JINX!" we shout, and then we crack up. We are *definitely* best friends.

"I'm fine," Lily says, "except my basketball flew way over the fence!"

I jump to my feet and brush myself off. "Well, I'm okay too," I say. "I'm sorry I crashed into you." Then I reach out my hand and help Lily. "Come on. Let's go find that basketball!"

We race around the fence to search through the bushes and check behind trees.

"Found it!" Jasmine cries.

Lily's basketball is sitting beside the old town well.

"Wow!" Posey exclaims. "I haven't seen one of these in *years!*"

"Seen one of what?" Lily asks. "A basketball?"

"No, *that!*" He points to the well. "Do you know what that is?"

"It's an old water well," I say, like no big whoop, because that well has been sitting here my whole life and

probably two lifetimes before that. It's made of stones and has a worn-out roof with weeds growing over it. I'm pretty sure the world forgot it existed.

Posey looks shocked. "It's not just *any* old well. It's a magic *wishing well*!"

Jasmine, Lily, and I stare at the old well and shrug. It sure doesn't look like anything special. But one thing is for sure—when Posey thinks something's magic, it usually is!

Obviously.

CHAPTER TWO

The Wishing Well

Posey whips out a coin, and it gleams in the sun.

"Watch this!" he says. Then he closes his eyes, *kisses the coin*, and flings it into the well.

PLINK! It plops into the water.

Posey opens his eyes and looks this way and that. Then he runs around the well twice and stops in front of us.

"That's really weird!" he says. "I made a wish, but my wish didn't come true!"

Jasmine covers her mouth to muffle a laugh. "Silly Posey!" she says. "The wishes don't actually come true!"

Lily and I nod in agreement.

"The best part of a wish is *wishing* it comes true," Lily says. Then she picks up a pebble and tosses it into the well.

Posey crosses his arms and looks upset.

"You didn't really expect your wish to come true, did you?" I ask.

"Of course I did!" he says with a little sass in his voice. "It's a *wishing well*! That's what wishing wells *do*!"

I peer down the old well. "Hmm . . . maybe this one's broken."

Posey's face lights up. "That's it!" he says, and before any of us can stop him, he starts kicking the outside of the well.

"POSEY!" I shriek. "You're going to break something!"

"No, I'm going to fix something!" says Posey.

Now my wacky imaginary friend is floating around the well, inspecting every stone. Then he flies into the woods with his eyes fixed on the ground. After a moment he picks up a small stone.

"Aha," Posey says with a grin. "This mystery is solved!"

He takes the stone and fits it back into the side of the well like a puzzle piece. Then everything around us begins to shudder and shake. I'm pretty sure the well is going to *erupt*. Lily, Jasmine, and I grab hold of one another. And then—*KER-FLOOSH!*

A gushing rainbow fountain blasts out of the well!

"POSEY, WHAT'S GOING ON?" I yell over the roar of magic.

He stands triumphantly and cheers, "I FIXED THE WISHING WELL!"

☆ Chapter Three ☆

The Wish List

We stare *inside* the rainbow. It's a rainbow of wishes! And we can actually *see* the wishes! Or at least, we can see the shapes of the wishes. I spy a pony, a tiara, tons of kittens and puppy dogs, several dolls, a trampoline, skateboards, swings, swimming pools . . . and much, much more.

"Wow!" Posey exclaims. "I've never

seen so many ungranted wishes in my imaginary life!"

I tap my goofball of a friend on the shoulder and ask, "Um, what do you mean, *ungranted* wishes?"

"These are all the wishes people made that never came true because

the well was broken," Posey says. "But it's not broken anymore! See?" Posey pulls an *enormous* butterscotch lollipop from behind his back and licks it. "I got my wish!"

And that's when I hear someone scream my name.

"*DAAAAAIIIISSSSSYYYYY!*"

I whirl around, and *OH. MY. GOSH.*
Lily is still Lily, but she is standing
next to a grown-up. And it isn't just
any grown-up. Because though she's
taller and has some gray in her hair, I
could never forget those kind eyes and
face. There's no doubt—this grown-up
is one of my best friends. "*JASMINE?*
What happened?" I ask. "What did
you wish for?"

Jasmine looks down at herself. "I'm
not sure!" she cries. "I haven't wished
for anything in a really *long* time."

Then Lily claps her hand over her

mouth. "Jasmine, don't you *remember?*
We made wishes at the well when we
were little, and you wished you were
a *grown-up!*"

Then Jasmine's eyes bug out, and
I know that she remembers, all right.

"Cool wish! Do you want to see
yourself?" Posey asks. He pulls a

mirror from out of nowhere and hands
it to Jasmine.

    Uh-oh, this is not going to be good, I
think. Then I cover my ears and wait
for it.

"*Aaaaaaaaaaaaaaaaaah!* I'm OLD!" Jasmine yells at the top of her lungs. "I look like my *mom!*" Then she turns and glares at Posey. "Please! Help me *unwish* it!"

Posey licks his lollipop like it's no big whoop.

Lily points at Posey and shakes her finger. "*Posey, you have* to fix this! RIGHT NOW!"

"But I *did* fix it!" he says, pointing to the wishing well. "And, by the way, *you're welcome!*"

Posey takes a little bow, but poor Jasmine drops to her knees and clasps her hands together.

"*Please!*" she begs. "I'm not a grown-up, Posey. I'm supposed to be a *kid!*"

But Posey's not paying attention to any of us. He has his mind on the well, which is now making a funny noise, like a printer.

ZA-ZINK! ZA-ZINK! ZA! ZINK! ZINK! ZINK!

A stream of paper spits out of the side of the wishing well. It looks like a super-long grocery store receipt, and it shows no sign of stopping. Posey collects the paper as it comes out.

"What is *that*?" I ask.

Again, no answer. Posey is concentrating on the spewing paper. Finally it stops, and he rips the end of the paper from the well.

"This is the wish list!" he tells us. "It shows every wish made at this well *and* the name of the person who wished it."

We watch Posey scroll down the long list.

"Ta-da!" he says triumphantly. "Here's Jasmine's wish to be a grown-up!" He bows his head toward Jasmine, who is still on her knees. "Congratulations! Your wish came true!"

And now I, Daisy Dreamer, have had *enough*. I march right over to Posey and speak to him in my best I-mean-business voice. "Posey, Jasmine

doesn't *want* to be a grown-up any- more. *Obviously!* So please hurry up and use your magic or whatever to help her become a normal kid again."

Posey stands there, scratching his head. "Oh dear. Now, that's going to be a problem because I don't know how to undo a wish."

I slap my hand against my forehead. "Oh no, Posey! This is *bad*! This is *really bad*!"

Then, right in the middle of losing it, I think of something *worse* than really bad . . . and I feel a wave of panic rush over my body.

"Posey, how many wishes on that list did you make come true?" I ask.

Posey glances at the list and then back at me. He drops his lollipop in the dirt when he realizes what he's really done by fixing the well.

"All the wishes in the well!" he says, his eyes growing wider. He gulps. "And that's a *lot* of wishes. This well has been broken for a long, long time."

I grab the list from his hand and look over the names. Then I find it— *my mom's name*! And of course she made the wish when she was a little girl.

"UH-OH!" I shout, flinging the wish list back at Posey. "We have to go to my house! And I mean, like, NOW!"

☆ CHAPTER FOUR ☆

Mom's Not-So-Little Pony

My friends and I *bolt* to my house, which suddenly feels a bazillion miles away. Posey flies. I whiz on my skateboard. Lily runs like the wind, and grown-up Jasmine scooters awkwardly. Her scooter is way too small for her now.

"I thought being a grown-up would make things easier," Jasmine complains. "But this isn't easy at all!"

I push harder to make my skateboard go faster. When we finally get home, Jasmine and Posey go in the front door and sneak straight up to my room. Lily and I race in through the back door.

"MOM!" I shout as soon as we're inside. "Is everything *okay*?"

My mom is stirring spaghetti sauce in the kitchen. She looks as normal as normal can be, except for that she has one eyebrow raised. "I'm fine, thank you," she says. "Are *you* okay, Daisy?"

Now it's my turn to act as normal as normal can be. "I'm fine, thank you too!" I say. And that's when we hear a loud noise upstairs.

WOMP! WOMP!

We all look at the ceiling.

"That's odd," Mom says. "I thought your father was at the grocery store."

I give Lily a look and say, "That's just Jasmine. She had to get something in my room."

Then I creep toward the hallway as more loud noises come from upstairs. *WUMP! WUMP! WUMP!*

This time the walls actually shake. I laugh nervously. "I guess it's a *big* something! Better go help her!"

Lily and I race out of the kitchen and bound up the stairs. When I fling open my bedroom door, it's just as I feared. There is a *pony* standing on what used to be my bed.

"Daisy, when did you get a pony?" asks grown-up Jasmine.

I sweep up my pigtails to cover my eyes, and then I let my hair drop back down. Nope, it didn't work. That pony is still there!

"I didn't!" I whisper-yell. "It's my mom's wish. When she was little, she wanted a pony. So she made a wish in the well. Now it's come true . . . and her wish is in my room!"

"This is so cool!" Lily says.

I glare at her. "How is this cool?"

I point around my room, which is

a *complete* disaster. My desk chair is smashed. My clothes are chewed, slobbered on, and scattered all over the floor. Even right now that pony is chewing on Cuddles, my stuffed moray eel. I throw my hands in the air.

"My room is not a barn!" I cry. "What are we gonna do now?"

Then I have an idea and smile at Jasmine.

"What are you looking at *me* for?" she asks.

"Because you are a grown-up!" I say. "And grown-ups usually know what to do!"

Jasmine smiles, and for one second she likes being a grown-up. She taps the side of her face with her finger to see if she has any grown-up ideas. Then *bing!* She's got one!

"We have to move the pony somewhere safe until we can reverse the wishing-well spell," she says.

I clap my hands because that's actually a very good idea. "Let's hide the pony at *school*!" I suggest.

Everyone stares at me like I'm a cuckoohead. Even the pony stops chewing.

"Guys, it's *the weekend*!" I explain. "School is over. Nobody will be around to see!"

Jasmine looks down at me like an adult when a kid gets a harebrained idea. "And how do you plan to get the pony out of your house and all the way to school?"

"Well, you can't expect me to work out *all* the details," I grumble. *Obviously.*

Posey steps up and raises his hand. "Leave the masterminding to *me*! Now, if you could all crowd around the pony."

We squeeze in, stepping over all the broken pieces that used to be my room.

Posey cheers, "GIBBIDY-GOOBIDY, TAKE-US-TO-SCHOOL-BIDDY!"

And with a clap of his hands— *POOF!* We disappear!

Chapter Five

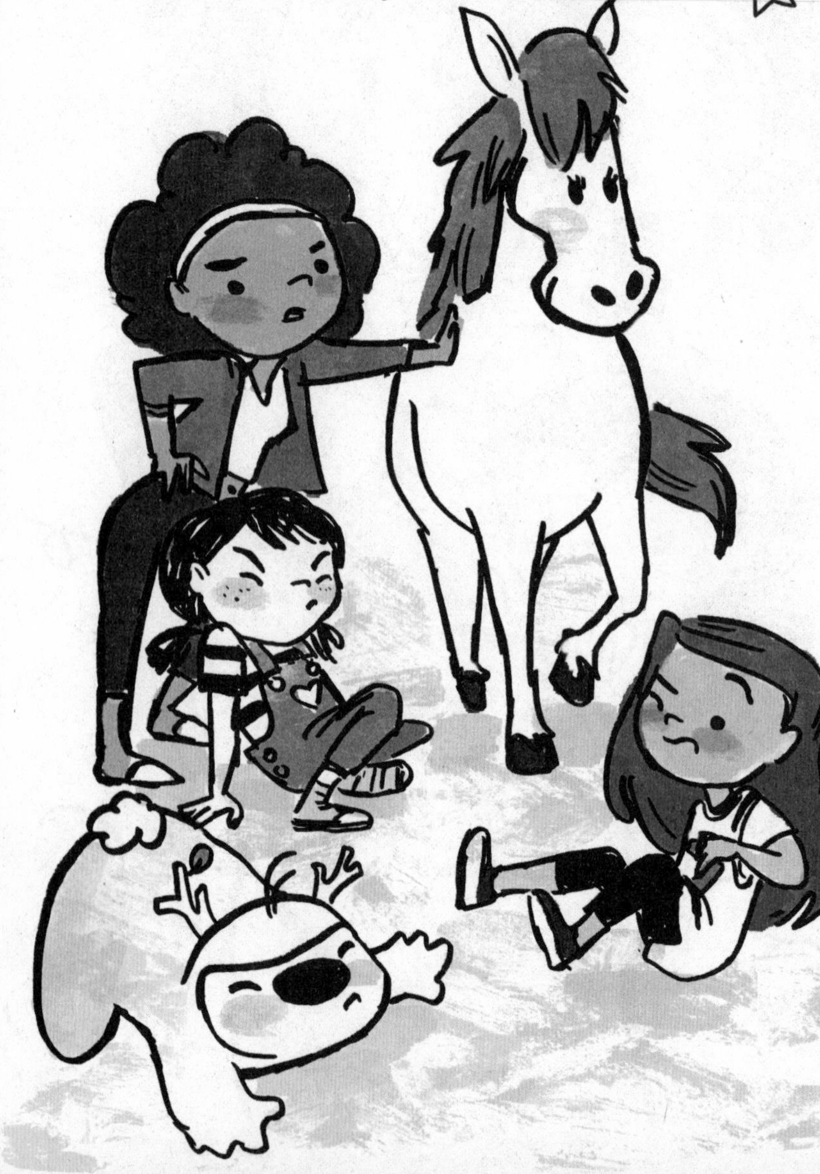

Princess Gabby

KER-SPLUNK! We land in an ungraceful heap on the ground—pony and all. I look around because I can't find our school anywhere. And then I realize there's a fairy-tale castle right where our school is supposed to be!

"What's *that* doing there?" I say, even though I know it must have something to do with the wishing well.

Jasmine gets to her feet. "Yeah, that's definitely not our school!"

Posey whips out the wish list. "Hmm . . . do you know anyone named Sterling Smith?"

We all nod because Sterling Smith goes to our school.

"Well, she wished kids would never have to go to school!" Posey says. "So now there's no school!"

Not an entirely bad wish, I think.

Then I ask, "Wait, whose castle is this?"

My question is answered by a blast of royal trumpets. We jump at the sound and see a team of knights galloping up to us. In the midst of the

knights is a princess on a tall white horse. She looks right at me.

"Well, well!" she says in a familiar voice. "If it isn't Miss Daisy Dreamer!"

I moan, because of course it's Gabby Gaburp, my best-worst enemy. She's even dressed like a fairy-tale princess!

Posey flies over and cups his hands around my ear to whisper, "Gabby wished to be a princess."

As if I didn't know. *OBVIOUSLY!*

Princess Gabby clears her throat to get our attention back on her. "*Ahem.* So, what are *you* doing here? And why do you have that beautiful pony?"

Oh wow, I forgot about the pony problem for a minute. Then I realize, *Hey, maybe Princess Gabby can help us.*

"Your Royal Highness," I begin, trying not to make a sour face at calling Gabby such a fancy name. "We have come to bring you a gift! This rare and

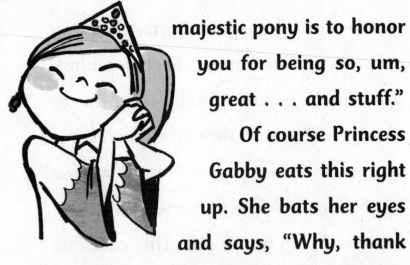

majestic pony is to honor you for being so, um, great . . . and stuff."

Of course Princess Gabby eats this right up. She bats her eyes and says, "Why, thank you, my faithful subject. Your Highness accepts your kind gift with pleasure."

Then she and her knights lead the pony away. "Pony problem solved!" I cheer as I bow to my friends like a magician.

Jasmine wipes her brow. "Good thinking, Daisy!"

"Phew," Lily agrees, leaning against a tree. That's when we notice that the tree Lily's leaning on . . . begins to *pop.*

Poppity! Poppity! POOF! The whole tree turns into *chocolate*—right before our eyes!

"How did you do that?" Jasmine exclaims.

Lily backs away from the tree in surprise. "Oh no! I just remembered my wishing-well wish."

"Lilyyy," I say, dragging her name out because I cannot believe what I think her old wish was. "Did you wish that everything you touched would turn to . . ."

Lily nods. "Chocolate."

Then she takes a big bite of the tree.

Chapter Six

Wish Disaster!

"Why did you wish that?" Jasmine says. "That's the silliest wish ever!"

Lily snaps off a twig from the chocolate tree. "Hmm . . . maybe not as silly as wishing to be a grown-up!"

Uh-oh! Angry best friend alert! This is not good! I try to lighten the mood. "I think Lily's wish is sweet! Get it? *Sweet!* Because she wished for chocolate!"

Lily sort of snort-laughs.

Then I stand up as tall as I can.

"I think Jasmine's wish is big. I mean,

who hasn't wanted to be a grown-up before?"

Jasmine sort of snort-giggles.

Now that everyone is smiling, I feel better. "They're both good wishes."

Jasmine shakes her head. "Good wish or not, it's starting to feel more like a curse!"

It's true, I think. A harmless wish can go bad *just like that*. Then I ask Posey for the wish list so I can look it over. It's scary to think that all these wishes have come true—at the *same time*.

I read them over and imagine what's going on all over town.

Oh wow! Gabby's best friend and main meanie, Carol Rattinger, wished she could talk to animals. *This is kind of a cool wish,* I think, except when she hears what her pets are thinking. Her cat is probably saying, "Get your hands off me, Carol!" or "Can I eat Swimmy, your goldfish?" or "Oops, I clawed a hole in your beanbag chair!" And Carol is probably covering her ears and screaming, "Be quiet, Furball!"

And oh gosh, John Gates, a boy in my class, wished he could fly. Now, that sounds like a great wish, but what if he can't come down to the ground anymore? What would his parents do? Tie him down like a helium balloon when it's time for dinner?

I shake my head and read another wish, and it is a *doozy*! Wren Sinclair, who's older than me, wished for a *million* cats. What was she thinking? A million cats mean a million cat *poops* every single day! I pinch my nose and read the next wish.

Great balls of flame-breath! Ashley Wyatt wished for a dragon. Doesn't she know dragons are a fire hazard? A dragon could burn down her house with one sneeze! Or scorch her best friend!

Jefferson Winthrop wished it was always summer. Now he'll never get to go sledding or make snow angels! Carlotta Gomez wished she were *in* a TV show. Now she's probably trapped inside her TV. And Tony Smalls, who lives on my street, wished he would never have to go to bed again. He'll probably turn into a *zombie*.

That's when I know that every wish has an upside and a downside. "Posey, I never thought I'd say this: We need to ruin everyone's wishes."

Posey salutes me, probably because I sound like General Crazypants. He quickly chants more magic words and claps. *POOF!* We disappear again.

Chapter Seven

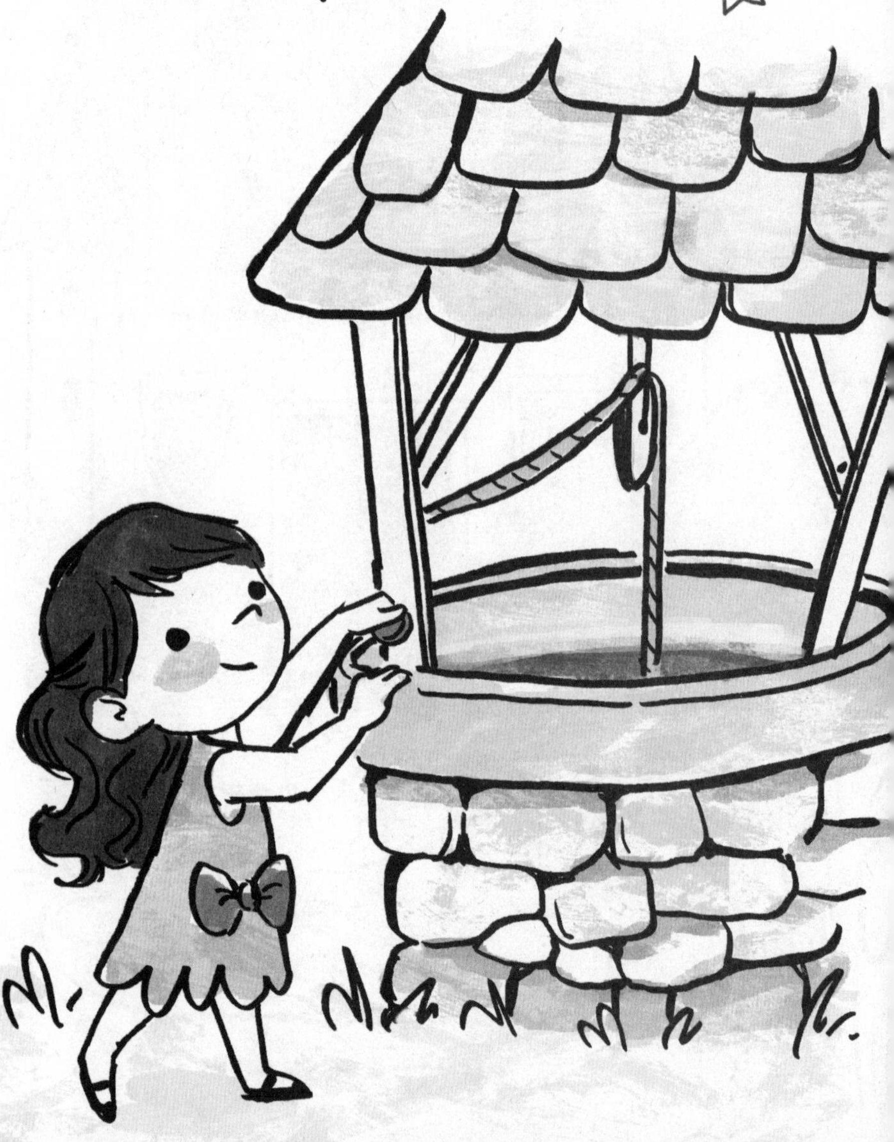

Turn It DOWN

This time we land on our feet next to the wishing well. And wouldn't you know, another girl is there too, with a coin in her hand. She's making a wish.

"WAIT!" we shout. But it's too late. The girl tosses her coin into the well.

PLINK! It splashes into the water. Immediately the girl begins to glow. Then *ZAP!* There's a flash of bright

light and now the girl looks totally dif-ferent. She's wearing a mask, a navy cape, and a pink costume.

She stands with her fists on her hips and announces, "It worked! I'm a superhero!"

Then she pumps her fist and flies away into the sky.

I turn to Posey. "You have to stop this wishing well! Can't you just pull out that stone you put back?"

"If I knew which stone it was." Posey pats around the side of the well.

Then he stops and says, "Hmm . . . I can't stop the wishes, but maybe I can dampen them."

Lily frowns. "Does that mean I have to eat damp chocolate?"

Posey rolls his eyes. "No, dampen as in lessen. Wishing wells have a switch to control the strength of the

wishes. We can turn down the strength like turning down the volume on loud music. For Lily, it would put a limit on what she turns into chocolate. For Jasmine, it might make her a teenager instead of a grown-up."

Jasmine and Lily give a thumbs-up to Posey's idea. Then we all help look for the switch.

Unfortunately, wishing-well switches are not easy to find. We get on our hands and knees and begin to uproot the overgrown weeds and vines. Posey pulls a vine with roots that go on for-ever. We all grab hold of it and pull

until we uncover a rusty metal plate
on the side of the well.

"That's it!" Posey cries.

Hmm, I bet that switch has not been used in a hundred years.

"Do you think it still works?" I ask.

"There's only one way to find out," says Posey. He flips the switch, and *WHOOSH!* Something definitely happens.

Chapter Eight

Oops!

Posey hops to his feet and dusts off his hands. Then he smiles and says, "That should do the trick!"

I gasp and point to Lily and Jasmine. "It did the trick, all right—in the opposite direction! You super-charged the wishes!"

Posey yelps. "Oh no! Jasmine, you're an old lady!"

Jasmine grabs a lock of her curly hair and screams. "It's GRAY!"

Whoa, one of my best friends now looks like she's my grandma Upsy's age!

"Posey, you turned the volume UP instead of DOWN!" I shout.

That's when we notice that everything around us is going crazy.

John Gates, the boy who wished he
could fly, is headed for *outer space*!

Wren Sinclair, the girl who wished for a million cats, is being chased by millions and trillions of cats. Oh meow, oh my!

Then that awful Carol Rattinger, who wished she could talk to animals, runs by and hides behind me. "Help me, Daisy! It's the squirrels! They know I can understand them, and now they won't leave me alone!"

Suddenly I look up, and we are sur-rounded by hundreds of squirrels in the trees and on the ground. And they are all squeak-chattering at Carol.

She screams back at them, "For the last time, I don't have any nuts!"

Here's the thing about squirrels: They are not good listeners. They keep squirrel-talking to Carol nonstop. With another shriek, Carol darts back into the park, and all the squirrels chase after her. On a regular day this might be the funniest thing I've ever seen in my life. But not today.

"Ugh. I don't feel so good," Lily

says, and boy, does she sound sick.

I swing around to see Lily standing as still as a statue . . . a chocolate statue! Everything from her neck
down has turned into delicious chocolate! I sure hope those
hungry squirrels
don't come back!

Now I have to
do something, so
I run to the well
and grab the
control switch.

And guess what
that old rusty switch

does? It breaks off in my hand. Oops.
I hold the switch up in the air to show
the others, as if to say, Okay, *we're*
officially cursed for all time.

During all the hoopla, Grandma

Jasmine shuffles over and picks up the wish list. "I think I might have a solution."

I wish, I think, and I freak out at my choice of words. Then I relax a tiny bit because Jasmine's voice sounds as calming as Upsy's. I hope she's as wise as Upsy too. "So, what's your idea?"

Old Jasmine chews on her wrinkly bottom lip. "I have to warn you, Daisy. You may not like it."

I raise my eyebrows. How could I not like a solution to this madness?

105

☆ Chapter Nine ☆

One Last Wish

Jasmine holds up the list. Her hand shakes. "Your name is not on the wish list," she says. "That means you've never made a wish at the wishing well."

She's right about that! I never have—and after today, I probably never will.

Jasmine smiles. "Don't you see, Daisy? You can save us with a wish!"

I frown because I've seen what wishes do.

Jasmine can tell I'm worried, so she calmly tells me, "The only downside is that you'll have to give up your one and only wish."

There's not much to think about because given a choice, I'd always pick

saving my friends, my town, and, yes, even my school. "Who has a coin?"

Posey shakes his head. "Sorry. I used my only coin for the wish lollipop."

Lily stands as still as a chocolate-dipped pretzel rod. "I have chocolate coins in my pocket. Will those work?"

I shake my head and look at Jasmine. She opens her coin purse and looks through it very slowly—like, super-old-person slowly.

"Hurry up!" I say, because I can see the shadow of Ashley's wish dragon flying way up in the clouds. And it's heading right for Princess Gabby's wish castle!

Then Jasmine holds up a penny and hands it to me.

I close my eyes, and—

"WAIT!" Posey yells. "Remember, don't say your wish out loud or it won't come true!"

Oh, brother, I think. *Obviously.* Then I close my eyes again, kiss the coin, and make my wish!

Plink!

Chapter Ten

NUTS!

Everything is back to normal—like, a kind of right-before-we-saw-Posey-and-I-crashed-into-Lily-and-Lily-lost-her-basketball normal. Nobody remembers anything about the wishing-well spell except me. I'm riding my skateboard. Lily's not made of chocolate and she's shooting hoops while young Jasmine draws on the ground with chalk.

"Do you want to play HORSE?" I shout as I whiz by my friends.

Jasmine looks up and says, "Sure!"

"Count me in!" agrees Lily.

We take turns shooting hoops. My shot hits the rim and bounces off the court.

"That's an *H*!" Jasmine says.

I run off the court to get the ball, but somebody else has already grabbed it.

"Posey!" I shout.

He tosses the ball to me and winks. "You must have wished a really good wish!"

I look back at the girls, and then I whisper, "Posey! You're not supposed to remember anything! That was part of my wish."

A sly grin spreads across his face. "I could never forget one of our adventures!" Then he looks around. "So, did you change everything back to normal?"

I bounce the basketball on the dirt. *"Almost everything."*

Suddenly Carol Rattinger runs past us. She's being chased by hundreds of squirrels. "HELP! HELP! These crazy critters won't leave me alone!"

Posey looks at me, shocked. "Daisy, you can't let Carol talk to animals!"

We watch as Carol runs farther into the park with a sea of fluffy tails going after her.

"Oh, she *can't* talk to animals," I explain. "But until tomorrow those squirrels will think she can understand every word they say. And that's just long enough to drive her *nuts!*"

Check out Daisy Dreamer's next adventure!

"Sweet dreams, Daisy Dreamer!" Mom and Dad say as they turn off the lights.

"Wait! I'm not *tired*!" I tell them, but the door clicks shut. I stare up at the glow-in-the-dark stars on my ceiling and yawn.

Then I hear a familiar voice. "I'm not tired either!"

Excerpt from *Posey, the Class Pest*

I squint my eyes to see in the dark. I wish I were a cat, like Sir Pounce, so I could have super-duper night vision.

"Posey?" I call out. "Is that you?" My heart is beating so super fast. Then I spy a light tracing a new imaginary door on my wall. The door swings open, and there's my imaginary friend, wearing a big silly grin on his face.

"Hi, Daisy!" he says.

I breathe a sigh of relief. "You scared me!"

He slaps his knee and laughs, like he thinks that's so funny. "Sorry. I heard you weren't tired. So, do you

Excerpt from *Posey, the Class Pest*

want to have an adventure?"

I open my mouth, and another *big fat* yawn rolls out. "Isn't it kind of late to start an adventure?" I ask.

Posey jumps onto my bed. "Not in the WOM!" he says.

The WOM is the World of Make-Believe. *Obviously.*

"We could go to Roller-Coaster Raceway!" Posey suggests. "Or Bouncy Town, which is a whole town made out of bounce houses!"

I get up on one elbow. That *does* sound fun . . . but my eyes feel *so* heavy. . . .

Excerpt from *Posey, the Class Pest*